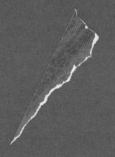

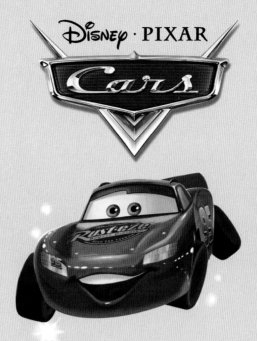

This special edition was printed for Kohl's Department Stores, Inc. (for distribution on behalf of Kohl's Cares, LLC, its wholly owned subsidiary), by Disney Press, New York/Los Angeles.

Kohl's
1224423-00
123387
09/14–10/14

Printed in China
First Edition
1 3 5 7 9 10 8 6 4 2
ISBN 978-1-4231-5138-8 • G615-7693-2-14286

For more Disney Press fun, visit www.disneybooks.com

DISNEY PRESS

New York • Los Angeles

The next morning, Mater the tow truck brought Lightning
to traffic court. The judge was an old car named Doc. When he
found out that Lightning was a race car, he told him to get out of
town. But a car named Sally disagreed. She wanted Lightning to
fix the road he had ruined.

Doc hesitantly agreed.

Doc ordered Lightning to fix the road, but Lightning refused. Doc challenged him to a race. "If you win, you go. If I win, you do the road my way."

Lightning agreed. He was sure he could beat the old car. But on a sharp left turn, Lightning lost control. He skidded off the road and plunged into a cactus patch.

Later that night, Lightning scraped the asphalt off the road. When the rest of the cars awoke the next morning, they saw Mater driving in circles on a section of perfectly smooth road.

Doc found Lightning at the site of their race. He was practicing his turns. But he kept losing control.

"This is dirt," Doc said. "You have to turn left to go right."

That night, Mater took Lightning tractor tipping. Mater snuck up on a sleeping tractor and honked. The startled tractor woke up and fell over.

When it was Lightning's turn, he revved his engine so loudly that all the tractors keeled over at one time. Mater and Lightning could not stop laughing. It had been a long time since Lightning had enjoyed himself that much.

The next morning, while Lightning waited for his daily gas ration, he wandered into Doc's shop. Suddenly, he noticed something on a shelf. A Piston Cup! Then he saw two more. Lightning couldn't believe it: Doc Hudson was the "Hudson Hornet"—a racing legend!

"Let's go for a drive," Sally suggested that afternoon.
Looking out over Radiator Springs, Sally explained that
it had once been a busy town. But no one had visited since
the Interstate had been built. Now everyone just went
around it on the way to somewhere else.

Later that day, as Lightning worked on the street, he saw Doc roaring around the dirt racetrack.

Lightning followed Doc to his office. "How could you quit at the top of your game?" he asked.

Doc showed Lightning a newspaper article about a wreck he had been in. By the time he was fixed, the world had forgotten about him.

The next morning, the road was finished. Although Lightning was free to go, he wasn't quite ready. First he stopped by each store. He filled up on Fillmore's organic fuel, tried out night-vision goggles at Sarge's Surplus Hut, picked out a bumper sticker at Lizzie's curios shop, bought new tires from Guido and Luigi, and got a new paint job at Ramone's House of Body Art.

Finally, it was time for Lightning to go.

Lightning made his way to California for his big race. But as the race started, Lightning couldn't concentrate. He kept remembering his friends in Radiator Springs. Somehow, winning no longer seemed that important.

Just then Doc's voice came over the radio: "I didn't come all this way to see you quit."

Lightning looked at his pit and saw all of his Radiator Springs friends. Doc was sitting on the crew-chief platform!

Lightning revved his engine and got back into the race.

Lightning tore around the track. He had fallen behind, but he knew he could catch up.

His opponent Chick Hicks tried to stop him with some dirty tricks, but Lightning remembered what his friends had taught him. He drove backward; he turned left to go right. And when he blew a tire, Guido performed the fastest tire change in history!

Finally, Lightning took the lead! Chick Hicks and The King were fighting for second place.

"I'm not coming in behind you again!" Chick shouted, ramming The King. The race car hit a wall and flipped.

When Lightning saw The King's crumpled body, he remembered Doc's final crash. The King had decided this would be his last race. Lightning couldn't let it end this way. He screeched to a stop inches from the finish line.

As Chick crossed the finish line, Lightning drove over to The King.

"What are you doing, kid?" Doc asked through the headset.

"I think The King should finish his last race," Lightning answered as he pushed The King over the finish line.

The crowd erupted in cheers.

Chick might have won the Piston Cup, but Lightning was the hero of the race!

Tex, the owner of the Dinoco oil company, approached Lightning. "How would you like to be the new face of Dinoco?" he asked.

Lightning politely refused. He was loyal to his original sponsor, Rust-eze. But he did ask Tex for one favor. . . .

Soon Lightning returned to Radiator Springs. He found Sally
at the old Wheel Well Motel.

"I thought I'd stop and stay awhile," he told her.

Just then, they heard someone wildly yelling, "Woo-hoo!"

It was Mater. Thanks to Lightning, he was fulfilling his dream of taking a helicopter ride.

Sally smiled. Then she turned and sped off down the mountain, with Lightning close behind. It looked as if Lightning had found his new home.